Rosie & the
Yellow Ribbon

by Paula DePaolo

Pictures by Janet Wolf

Little, Brown and Company

Boston   Toronto   London

Text copyright © 1992 by Paula DePaolo
Illustrations copyright © 1992 by Janet Wolf

First Edition

Library of Congress Cataloging-in-Publication Data

DePaolo, Paula.
    Rosie and the yellow ribbon / by Paula DePaolo ;
pictures by Janet Wolf. — 1st ed.
    p.   cm.
    Summary: Although it was her favorite hair
ribbon, Rosie learns that her friendship with Lucille
means more to her than the missing yellow ribbon.
    ISBN 0-316-18100-5
    [1. Friendship — Fiction.]   I. Wolf, Janet, 1957–
ill.   II. Title.
PZ7.D4388Ro   1992
[E] — dc20   90-45689

Joy Street Books are published by
Little, Brown and Company (Inc.)

10 9 8 7 6 5 4 3 2 1

WOR

Published simultaneously in Canada
by Little, Brown & Company (Canada) Limited

Printed in the United States of America

To my parents, with love.
And to Bob, Adam, and Alex,
my three best friends.
— P. D.

For my dear friend Dr. Anne Peters
— J. W.

Rosie sat on the warm front steps of the apartment building where she lived. Next to her she had placed twenty brand-new hair ribbons, side by side like crayons in a box. They were a gift from her grandmother who lived far away. There were wide ribbons and narrow ribbons, satin ribbons and lacy ribbons. Some ribbons were checkered. Some had stripes. And one, a sunny yellow ribbon, had tiny white polka dots sprinkled all over it. That was Rosie's favorite.

"Good morning, Rosie," called Mr. Brown from across the street. "A little bird told me today is your birthday."

Rosie smiled and waved. "I'm six," she announced.

Mr. Brown unlocked the door to his grocery store and went inside. Wearing a crisp white apron, he stepped out to throw seeds to the sparrows who perched on his sign.

"Come see me later and we'll celebrate," he called to Rosie. Then he greeted his first customers of the day and followed them into the store.

Rosie saw her best friend, Lucille, coming down the street. Lucille would love the ribbons, too. She never wore ribbons in her hair. Her mama made bows out of yarn. Carefully, Rosie gathered the ribbons. Lucille would be so surprised.

"Happy birthday," said Lucille as she plopped down next to Rosie.

Rosie held out her ribbons. "Lucille, look!"

"O-o-oh, you're so lucky!" Lucille cried.

"Nanny sent them for my birthday," said Rosie. She lined up the ribbons on the steps again. "You can have one if you want."

Lucille reached for the yellow ribbon with the tiny white polka dots.

"Except that one," added Rosie. "That's my favorite."

"Rosie," called Mama from the upstairs window. "Nanny is on the telephone."

"Be right back," Rosie told Lucille as she bounded up the steps to her apartment. The cozy rooms were filled with the smell of chocolate. Chocolate cake and chocolate icing. A birthday cake to share with Lucille.

Mama handed her the phone.

"Uh-huh. Uh-huh. Thank you. I will. Bye, Nanny. I love you, too."

Rosie gave Mama a hug, then hurried down the steps to Lucille. But something was wrong. The ribbons were all messed up, and Lucille was gone.

So was the sunny yellow ribbon.

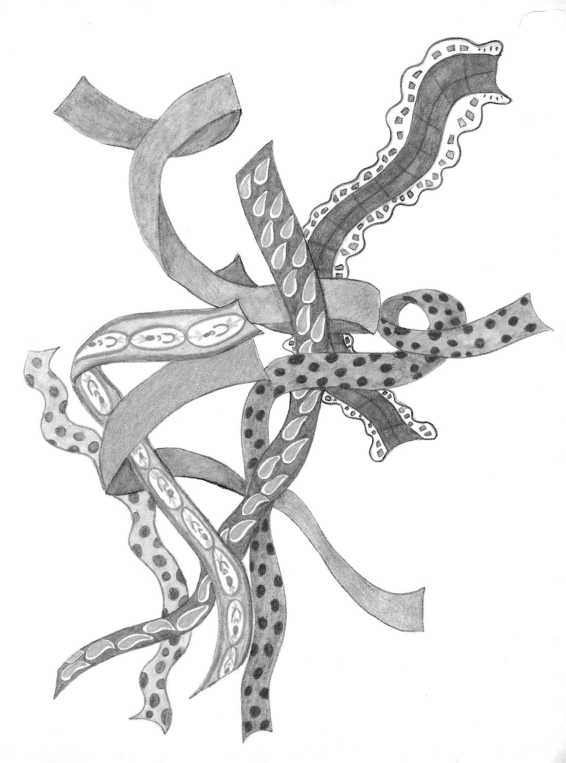

Rosie searched every step. She checked each square of sidewalk and peered down the dark sewer drain. Her favorite ribbon had disappeared, and she had never once worn it.

"What's the matter?" asked Lucille as she turned the corner. "Did you lose something?"

"Yes!" cried Rosie. "My yellow ribbon!"

"Where'd it go?" asked Lucille, looking around Rosie's stoop.

"Maybe someone took it," Rosie said, looking straight at Lucille.

"Who? Me?" said Lucille. "I did

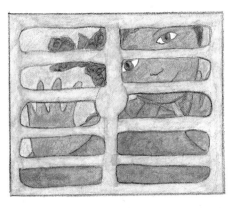

not! I went to open the door for Mrs. Wiggins. Her arm's broke."

"Then where's my ribbon?" asked Rosie. "It was right on that step."

"I don't know!" cried Lucille. "But I didn't take it!"

"Well, I left it with you and now it's gone. You better give it back, Lucille, or else you can't have any of my birthday cake."

Lucille planted her hands on her hips. "So what?" she said. "I don't like birthday cake anyway. And I don't want your ugly yellow ribbon!" Then she turned and ran home.

Rosie was sure Lucille would return right away with the yellow ribbon. But when it was time to blow out the candles on the cake, she still had not come back.

It felt strange having birthday cake without Lucille. And it wasn't much fun at Mr. Brown's — he had made a bowl of popcorn big enough for three.

"Maybe tomorrow," said Mr. Brown. But tomorrow came, and still Lucille had not returned.

All that day Rosie played with her ribbons until they were limp and smudged. She tied them on ponytails and braids, and after lunch she wore all nineteen at once. She thought a lot about the sunny yellow ribbon. But mostly she thought about Lucille.

The next afternoon Mr. Brown celebrated Monday. He treated Rosie to a lemonade at the counter. Next to her sat a fat bald man. He didn't talk or laugh or spin on
his seat the way Lucille did. He didn't even make slurpy noises with his straw.
Rosie slid off her stool and went home. She didn't feel like celebrating anymore.

From her window she watched the sparrows that lived on Mr. Brown's sign. She could see one of the birds as it flew in and out of the nest.

Rosie remembered how every morning she and Lucille had fed the sparrows crumbs, and how in the warm afternoons they had sat on Rosie's steps and waited for them to lay their eggs.

"It shouldn't be long now," Mr. Brown had told them, and he knew all about birds. A few days later, the first tiny egg had appeared in the nest.

That evening, when Rosie went to Mr. Brown's for her mother, she listened for the *cheep, cheep, cheep* of baby sparrows.

"Not yet," said Mr. Brown as he packed her mother's bread and milk into a bag. "But this afternoon I counted three speckled eggs."

On the way home, Rosie saw Lucille watching the sparrows from her window. It would have been fun to watch them together, Rosie thought. Everything was more fun with Lucille.

Suddenly, Rosie waved. But Lucille didn't wave back. Rosie waved again.

"Hi!" she called in a loud voice.

Lucille didn't answer. She just turned and walked away.

Rosie made a decision. Tomorrow she'd tell Lucille she could keep the yellow ribbon.

The next morning a blustery storm ripped through the city. Heavy rains flooded the streets and beat like pebbles against the windows. The wind howled through the narrow alleys and blew the rain this way and that. A dustbin rattle-clanked down the street, and a blue umbrella bounced along the pavement.

Rosie sat at her window, her nose pressed against the glass. She could barely see the nest through the pouring rain. She wondered if Lucille was watching, too.

Suddenly a gust of wind snatched the ragged nest and tossed it onto the awning. Down, down, it sailed to the slippery edge. Rosie's heart pounded as she saw the nest topple and fall, landing in the middle of Mr. Brown's petunias.

Rosie dashed down the stairs and out the door.

"Look both ways," her mother called after her.

Lucille was already outside and running towards Mr. Brown's shop.

"Lucille, wait!" called Rosie as she ran to catch up.

Together they crossed the deserted street and banged on Mr. Brown's door.

"Mr. Brown!" called Rosie.

"Hurry!" begged Lucille.

The sparrows looked down from the sign as Mr. Brown scooped up the cup-shaped nest and carried it to the safety of his doorway. Rosie and Lucille followed close behind.

"Are the eggs still there?" asked Rosie, standing on tiptoe.

"Did they get smashed?" asked Lucille, trying to peek inside.

"Hmmm," said Mr. Brown as he examined the wet nest. "My, my."

"There won't be any baby birds!" cried Rosie.

"See for yourselves," said Mr. Brown, cradling the nest in his hands.

Rosie and Lucille peered at the nest. They saw bits of string and twigs, feathers and leaves, all woven together. And down at the bottom sat three speckled eggs, nestled safely on a yellow ribbon with tiny white polka dots sprinkled all over it.

Rosie felt her cheeks grow hot.

"*There's* your yellow ribbon," said Lucille. "I told you I didn't take it."

Rosie stared at her wet trainers and tried to think of what to say. At last she said quietly, "I'm sorry, Lucille."

"That's okay," Lucille answered.

"Well," said Mr. Brown, "I think this calls for a celebration!" And when he had safely tucked the nest back on the sign, he poured three frosty glasses of lemonade.

As they headed home, Rosie asked Lucille, "Do you want to come to my house?
I saved you a piece of chocolate birthday cake."

"Yum," said Lucille. "I *love* chocolate birthday cake. And guess what? I still have your present."

"You have?" asked Rosie. "What is it?"